Professor McQuark
and the
Oojamaflip

Lou Treleaven
& Julia Patton

Professor McQuark has a marvellous brain,
as big as her head and half bigger again.

So crammed full of notions and thoughts and ideas,
they fill up her mind and pour out of her ears.

Like wind-up pet goldfish
that swim through the air,

and dice that are nice to you
if you play fair,

and rainbows that paint if
you give them a squeeze,

and tissues that bless you whenever you sneeze.

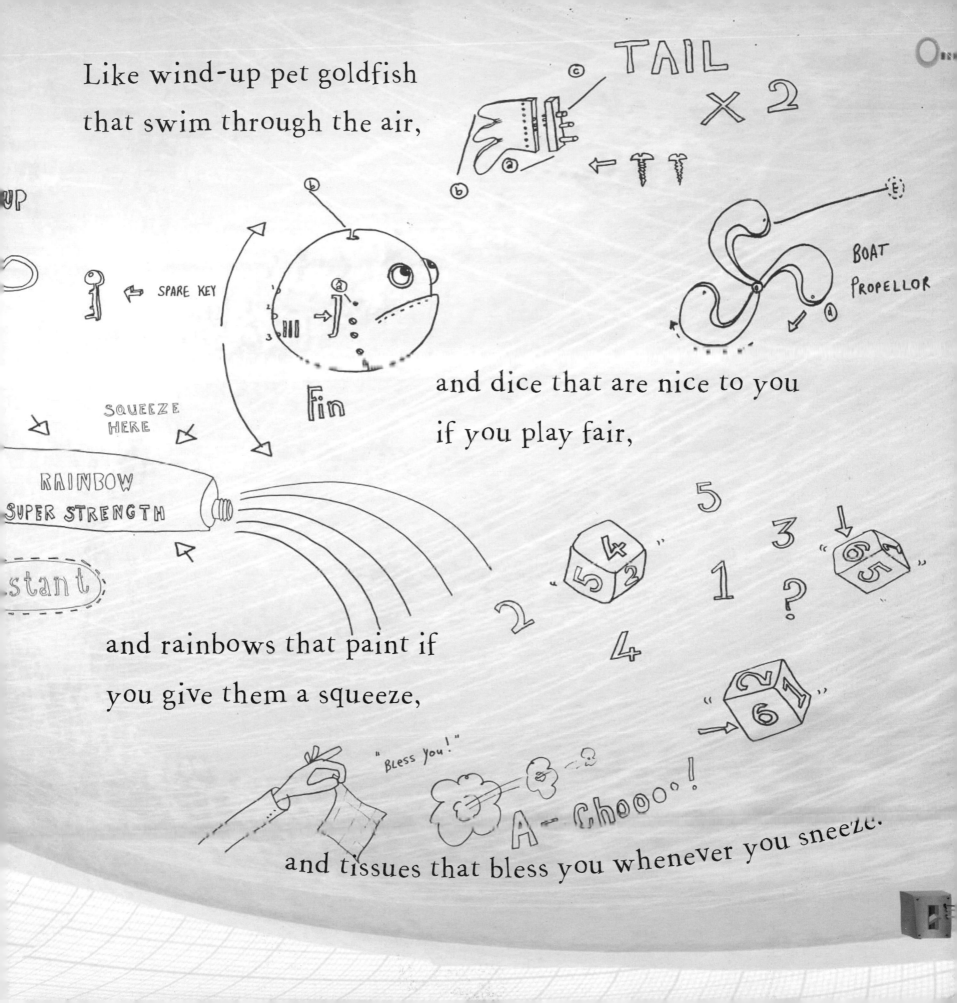

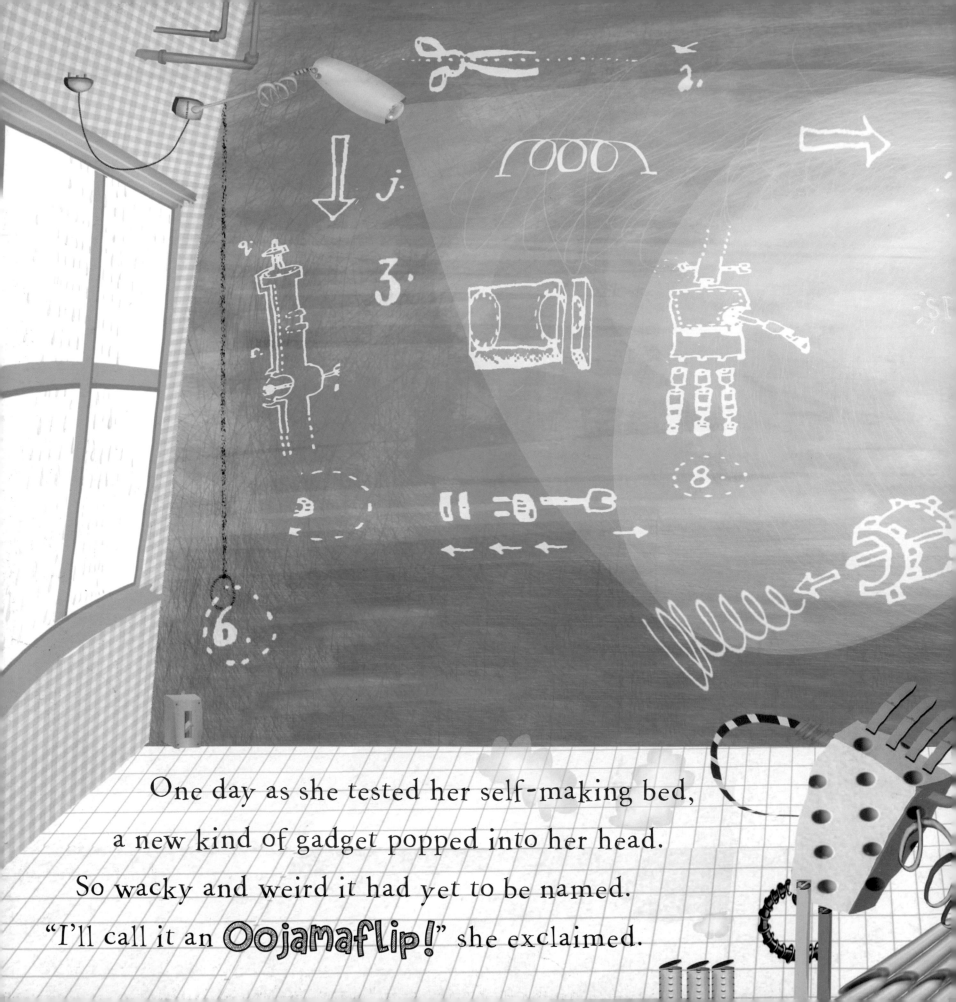

One day as she tested her self-making bed,
a new kind of gadget popped into her head.
So wacky and weird it had yet to be named.
"I'll call it an Oojamaflip!" she exclaimed.

She ran to her shed and she banged and she battered,

she sawed and she sanded, she clanged and she clattered.

She wound up the engine and honked on its horn.

At long last the Oojamaflip had been born!

Now every new product that shows special flair,
is put on display at the town's Science Fair.
So Professor McQuark gave the headlights a polish
and set off prepared to astound and astonish.

She reached the town hall with just one tiny flaw:
the **Oojamaflip** would not fit through the door!

"Too big," sighed the Prof, so she told it to park,
and into the fair went Professor McQuark.

The Science Fair buzzed with the hum of invention,
with gadgets of every shape, size and dimension.

From all round the globe, from the poles to next door,
there were novelties, knick knacks and wonders galore.

There were square balloon makers, a self-playing flute,

a yo-yo with slo-mo, a door with a zip,

a one-size-fits-all-humans alien suit,

but nothing as fine as the Oojamaflip.

The judges arrived looking earnest and wise,
to pick an invention to win the first prize.

scritch
scratch

BOING

ck
ck

Inspecting each one with a quizzical look,
they scratched little notes in a tiny gold book.

SPLAT

PiNg

"The judging is over," said one with a hat.

"The Square Balloon Makers have won. That is that.

But where have the people who visited gone?

They have all run outside - what on earth's going on?"

The judges went out. The Professor ran after.

They followed the honking of horns and of laughter.

 entions

Medium Inv

The children called out as they crowded around:
"just look at this wonderful thing we have found!"

This way up

"This **Oojamaflip**," said the judges, "is rare.
We see why the folk have assembled to stare.

ⓐ

We love the spare deckchair attached to the back,

ⓑ

and the doughnuts on ropes for a drive-along snack.

The grassy lawn seats are a treat we're admiring.

The paddling pool on the roof is inspiring.

The stained glass rear windscreen's a marvel it's true,

but what does this **Ooja-thing** actually do?"

"The clue's in the title," explained the Professor.
"A name such as this would suggest nothing lesser."
Professor McQuark put her hands on her hips.

"What does it do...?

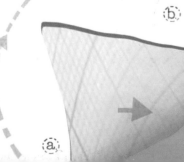

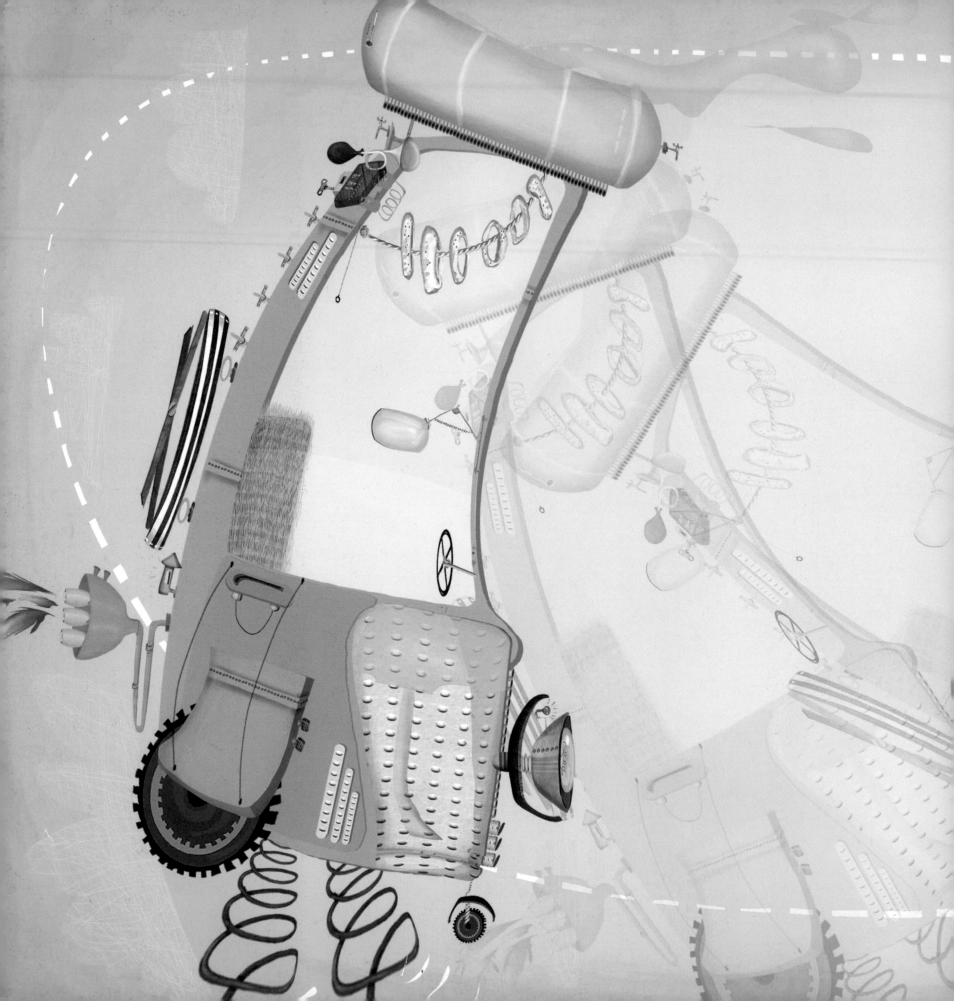

Professor McQuark and the Oojamaflip
An original concept by author Lou Treleaven
© Lou Treleaven

Illustrations by Julia Patton
Julia is represented by The Bright Agency
www.thebrightagency.com

Published by MAVERICK ARTS PUBLISHING LTD
Studio 3a, City Business Centre, 6 Brighton Road,
Horsham, West Sussex, RH13 5BB, +44 (0) 1403 256941
© Maverick Arts Publishing Limited January 2016

A CIP catalogue record for this book is available at the British Library.

ISBN: 978-1-84886-188-6

Maverick
arts publishing

www.maverickbooks.co.uk